MARTY FRYE PRIVATE EYE
THE CASE OF THE STOLEN POODLE
& OTHER MYSTERIES

FRYE

THE CASE OF THE STOLEN POODLE

& OTHER MYSTERIES

JANET TASHJIAN

illustrated by **LAURIE KELLER**

Christy Ottaviano Books

Henry Holt and Company • New York

Henry Holt and Company
Publishers since 1866
175 Fifth Avenue
New York, New York 10010
mackids.com

Henry Holt® is a registered trademark of Macmillan Publishing Group, LLC.
Text copyright © 2017 by Janet Tashjian
Illustrations copyright © 2017 by Laurie Keller

Library of Congress Cataloging-in-Publication Data

Names: Tashjian, Janet, author. | Keller, Laurie, illustrator.
Title: Marty Frye, private eye: the case of the stolen poodle / Janet Tashjian,
    illustrated by Laurie Keller.
Other titles: Case of the stolen poodle
Description: First edition. | New York : Henry Holt and Company, 2017. | Series:
    Marty Frye, private eye | Summary: Seven-year-old Marty Frye is on the job
    again, speaking in rhyme as he solves three new mysteries for the school nurse,
    the candy store owner, and a neighbor.
Identifiers: LCCN 2016037267 | ISBN 9781627794602 (hardcover)
Subjects: | CYAC: Mystery and detective stories. | Lost and found possessions—Fiction.
Classification: LCC PZ7.T211135 Maw 2017 | DDC [Fic]—dc23
LC record available at https://lccn.loc.gov/2016037267

Our books may be purchased in bulk for promotional,
educational, or business use. Please contact your local bookseller
or the Macmillan Corporate and Premium Sales Department
at (800) 221-7945 ext. 5442 or by e-mail at
MacmillanSpecialMarkets@macmillan.com.

First Edition—2017 / Designed by April Ward

Printed in the United States of America by
LSC Communications, Crawfordsville, Indiana

1 3 5 7 9 10 8 6 4 2

For Jake, another true poet.

—J. T.

To the Talented Tashjians,
Janet and Jake

—L. K.

CONTENTS

THE CASE OF THE ANGRY NURSE

THE CRIME

Marty Frye was standing at the water fountain when Billy ran down the hall and almost knocked him over.

Nurse Laughlin's on the warpath again!

Marty liked the new school nurse but agreed that she sometimes had quite the temper.

There's nothing worse than an angry nurse.

Billy rolled his eyes. "Do you have to rhyme all the time? Can't you just talk like a regular kid?"

Of course Marty COULD talk without rhyming, but if you're a poet detective, rhyming is part of the job.

"I make up rhymes while I solve crimes," Marty answered.

"Then you better get to Nurse Laughlin's," Billy said. "Because she's been robbed."

Marty skidded into the nurse's office. He found Nurse Laughlin collapsed on one of the beds usually reserved for sick students. Her face was as red as the cough drops she handed out during flu season.

Someone STOLE my tongue depressors!

3

"They were here yesterday but now they're gone," Nurse Laughlin said.

Marty knew he had to take notes if he was going to find Nurse Laughlin's missing equipment. He took out the spiral notebook he used to solve all his crimes.

This crime is horrific—please be specific.

"I've been trying to keep everything clean and organized." Nurse Laughlin pointed to the shelves, which were neat as a pin. "Why would someone want to steal tongue depressors?" She was **NOT** happy.

Marty wrote down everything Nurse Laughlin said. It was time to get busy.

Nurse Laughlin took a cloth from her cabinet and ran it under the faucet. She lay down and placed the cloth on her forehead. "There are some things only a cold compress can cure," she said.

While Nurse Laughlin was resting, Marty took out his magnifying glass to get a closer look around the office.

He opened the cupboard and found five boxes of bandages.

He found squares of gauze and jars of cotton balls.

He found lots of papers in the wastebasket.

He found swabs and inhalers and allergy medicine—but no tongue depressors.

When he approached Nurse Laughlin on the examining table, she jumped up with a start.

While I'm on my quest, you stay here and rest.

Nurse Laughlin no longer looked angry, but tired. "I'm just trying to run a sensible office," she said.

"I've got a hunch I'll solve this by lunch." Nothing would make Marty happier than getting Nurse Laughlin back on her feet—with her tongue depressors.

Nurse Laughlin gave Marty a hall pass so he could continue snooping.

The first place Marty decided to look was the art room. He remembered making log cabins out of sticks in Ms. Paquette's class last year. Could someone have taken Nurse Laughlin's tongue depressors to use for an art project?

Ms. Paquette must've been in another part of the building because her classroom was empty. It was the perfect time for Marty to snoop around.

HALL PASS

He searched through bins of crayons.
He sorted through stacks of construction
paper. He looked at the empty glass jars
and the sinks filled with bowls of water.
The tongue depressors were nowhere to
be found. He left the art room without
a clue.

When his classmate Emma asked where he was going, Marty told her about the theft in the nurse's office.

"I have recess next," she said. "Can I help?"

Did Emma think she was going to be his new sidekick? But even Marty had to admit that being a detective could be a lonely job. He decided to take her up on her offer.

You're my **chum**— of course you can come.

Marty felt a little nervous as they headed down the hall. The clock was ticking and all he had so far were dead ends.

Marty looked outside to the playground.
Several of his classmates were
playing tag and climbing on the jungle gym.

Maybe we should go outside
before we look for clues.

13

Didn't Emma know better than to suggest such a crazy idea?

I can't have fun till my work is done.

"OUR work," Emma added.

Marty noticed Joe from another class working in the school garden. He remembered when Joe asked for volunteers during their last assembly. Emma followed Marty outside.

Joe leaned on his shovel and pointed to several plants. "These are carrots, radishes, lettuce, and tomatoes. We're harvesting them to make salads for school lunches."

While Emma admired the plants, Marty examined the handmade signs sticking out of the dirt. He asked Joe who made them.

"I did," Joe said proudly. "Drew the pictures myself."

Enough with your tricks— you glued them on sticks!

Marty yanked one of the signs out of the ground. (The word "radish" was spelled wrong.)

Joe grabbed the sign away from Marty.

Of course I used sticks—how else would they stay in the ground?

Just as Marty was about to ask Joe where he got the sticks, Coach Martin blew his whistle signaling recess was over. Marty tried to question Joe further but Coach Martin guided them inside. Joe raced back to class before Marty could catch up.

"We can question Joe after class," Emma said. "But I think we should keep looking."

Marty was frustrated that his lead had fizzled out. He and Emma checked in on Nurse Laughlin who was still resting. And complaining. And resting.

"I guess it's a big deal when your tongue depressors go missing," Emma whispered to Marty.

"It might be traumatic, but she's too dramatic." Marty suggested they try the library.

Marty liked the librarian, Ms. Stanton. She used funny voices during Book Talks and had quotes from her favorite picture books painted on the walls. It was tempting to plop down in the story corner and grab one of his favorite books, but Marty took his detective job seriously.

With Emma's help, he scanned the shelves.

"Sometimes kids put things between books to remember their place," Emma said. "I found a few pencils but no tongue depressors."

But Marty had something else on his

mind as he checked out Ms. Stanton's desk. He removed several bookmarks from the wicker basket. The bookmarks were wooden sticks wrapped in colorful yarn. Ms. Stanton couldn't be involved—or could she? Marty asked the assistant librarian where Ms. Stanton was.

"She's preparing for an author visit," Mr. Malloy said. "She'll be back soon."

Marty didn't want to believe Ms. Stanton was the thief, but the evidence was overwhelming.

Marty and Emma hurried down the hall for a quick break before questioning Ms. Stanton.

It's time for a snack— I'll be right back.

Marty peeled his orange and handed a section to Emma. They were waiting outside Joe's classroom to ask him about the signs in the garden.

"They sure looked like the missing tongue depressors to me," Emma said. "I don't think Nurse Laughlin's going to be happy."

"I'm sure she'll be hurt if they're covered in dirt," Marty agreed.

Their friend Tammy came out of the classroom first. She called Emma over.

Look at the bracelet
I made in art class!

Emma told Tammy she had art later in the day and couldn't wait to make a bracelet too. Marty rolled his eyes—how could Emma be talking about jewelry at a time like this?

When Joe came out, Marty told him that Nurse Laughlin's tongue depressors had gone missing and that they looked exactly like Joe's signs.

"I bought my sticks at the craft store," Joe said. "My sister drove me there last night."

Marty didn't believe him—until Joe pulled out a crumpled receipt from his pocket. "You owe me an apology, Marty." Joe crossed his arms and waited.

I beg your pardon—I was wrong about your garden.

Before Joe could accept his apology, Marty took off down the hall when he spotted Ms. Stanton. If Joe wasn't the culprit, maybe their beloved librarian DID commit this crime.

Marty and Emma waited while Ms. Stanton answered the phone. Marty wasn't looking forward to questioning his favorite librarian.

Because he was a good detective, Marty noticed that Emma was now wearing Tammy's bracelet.

"She's letting me borrow it," Emma said. "I can't wait to make my own."

Marty examined the bracelet on Emma's wrist. Did Ms. Paquette let the students use metal in class now? He was surprised to find the bracelet was made of something else.

Emma gave Marty the bracelet just as Ms. Stanton hung up the phone.

"And how can I help two of my favorite students today?" the librarian asked.

But Marty and Emma were already halfway to the art room.

Ms. Paquette's class was lined up at the sink filling bowls of water. Ms. Paquette took a box out of a large bag. The box was labeled TONGUE DEPRESSORS.

Marty turned to Emma and pointed to the stolen sticks.

Here's where they went—but now they are bent!

Ms. Paquette took a tongue depressor out of the box. "If you soak these sticks for a few hours, you can bend them into lots of things." Ms. Paquette demonstrated by slipping a wet tongue depressor against the top of a jar. After a few minutes, the stick was bent into a semicircle.

Marty asked Ms. Paquette why she hadn't asked Nurse Laughlin for permission.

"Our last nurse always ordered extra tongue depressors and would let me have some. Since Nurse Laughlin is new, I left a note on her desk explaining what I

was using them for. I'm so sorry she
was upset."

Marty borrowed Tammy's bracelet and
went to tell Nurse Laughlin the news.

A JOB WELL DONE

Nurse Laughlin wasn't too happy her tongue depressors were now painted and bent like pretzels. "I can't put these in students' mouths." She studied the bracelet more closely. "It is pretty, though, isn't it?"

She gave the bracelet back to Marty.

"But I do wish the art teacher had asked first."

Marty rummaged through the wastebasket near Nurse Laughlin's desk that he'd looked in earlier. He took out a sheet of paper and held it up to Nurse Laughlin.

Nurse Laughlin read the note from Ms. Paquette asking for permission to use the tongue depressors. After that, she had to lie back down with another cold compress.

"I was so busy keeping my office neat that I cleared papers off my desk before reading them."

Nurse Laughlin thanked Marty for solving the mystery then filled out an order for more tongue depressors. She even ordered an additional box for Ms. Paquette. On the way to return the bracelet to Tammy, Marty ran into Billy.

Are you happy you solved your crime?

All this crime solving had made Marty hungry. The next mystery was figuring out what the cafeteria was serving for lunch.

2

THE CASE OF THE STOLEN CANDY

THE CRIME

On the walk home from school, Marty took off his backpack and climbed his favorite tree. The giant maple had lots of thick branches. From his perch, Marty had a great view of the park, town hall, fire station, pizza parlor, candy store, and pet shop. Lots of people were gathered at the fire station, probably for a field trip.

Aren't you that poet detective?

Marty looked down from his perch to see Mr. Hammond from the candy store.

"My famous hot jawbreakers have been stolen! Hundreds of dollars' worth— GONE!" Mr. Hammond said.

Marty scrambled out of the tree. His afternoon break would have to wait.

Marty followed Mr. Hammond to the candy store. It was one of his favorite places, with rows and rows of colorful penny candy. Lollipops, gum, candy necklaces, licorice, and fudge. The store carried everything a kid with a sweet tooth could want.

Marty took out his notebook. "I'm here to snoop—so give me the scoop."

Mr. Hammond nervously wrung his apron as he spoke. "Felix Dupont, the food critic from the local paper, is coming to write an article about the store—

especially our super hot jawbreakers. What
am I going to do? I ran to the bank and
when I came back, all the jawbreakers
were gone."

Marty popped a lemon sourball into his mouth. If he was going to solve this crime, he'd need to study the evidence.

Marty checked the locks on both doors but neither was broken. He asked Mr. Hammond if a customer might be involved instead of a burglar.

"The only customer I have trouble with is Jerome. He tries to sneak candy into his pockets all the time." Mr. Hammond looked around the store. "But I never thought he'd take every last jawbreaker."

Marty wrote this fact into his notebook. He also continued to look around the store. Something was definitely wrong.

Marty pointed to the tile floor. It was perfectly neat, with no sign of discarded wrappers.

This place is clean for a robbery scene.

Mr. Hammond didn't have time to answer Marty because a tall man with a beard and a tape recorder entered the store. Mr. Hammond pulled Marty aside. "It's Felix Dupont from the town paper— and I don't have any jawbreakers!"

The critic introduced himself to Mr. Hammond and Marty. He asked if the photographer had arrived yet. Mr. Hammond said no and led the critic to the fudge.

From his place behind the chocolate coins, Marty spied on Mr. Dupont.

The food critic was also writing in a spiral notebook. But even with that in common, Marty wasn't sure he trusted this guy. Did Mr. Dupont know more about Mr. Hammond's store than he was letting on?

Just as Marty was about to question the food critic, a woman burst into the candy shop carrying a fancy bag. It was Nancy Bowman from the comic book

store across the street. Ever since Mrs. Bowman started selling treats alongside her comic books, she and Mr. Hammond had been in a candy feud. (Marty had already made a note to question Mrs. Bowman and was disappointed that now he wouldn't get to visit her store—and her comic books.)

As soon as Mr. Hammond spotted his competition, he guided Mrs. Bowman out the door.

Now is not the time. I've got an important guest to entertain.

"That's why I'm here!" Mrs. Bowman turned right around and came back in.

She introduced herself to Mr. Dupont and handed him the fancy striped bag. "My store is right across the street," she said. "And you simply *must* sample these new ginger squares!"

Marty wondered if Mrs. Bowman was offering the hot jawbreakers  alongside the ginger squares in her store.

The food critic popped one of the candies into his mouth. "Delicious! I will certainly visit your store when I'm done."

"This is a disaster!" Mr. Hammond whispered to Marty. "Felix is here to write about my hot jawbreakers, not her ginger squares!"

Out of the corner of his eye, Marty spotted a kid near the yogurt-covered pretzels. It was Jerome with the bottomless appetite for goodies.

Are you here to eat this yogurty treat?

'Cuz you won't be successful at stealing that pretzel.

(The only thing that made Marty happier than solving a case was using a double rhyme.)

Jerome took a step away from the counter but still kept his eye on the treats. Mr. Hammond looked like he was in the middle of a full-blown panic attack.

Making sure his clients stayed calm was an important part of a detective's job. Marty had to find a clue—and **fast**.

THE SEARCH CONTINUES

If Jerome had stolen Mr. Hammond's jawbreakers, why did he return to the scene of the crime?

"If you made a score, why come back for more?" Marty asked.

I didn't steal anything. I love this place.

"I think you should ask Mrs. Bowman—all she does is complain that everyone in town likes Mr. Hammond's store more than hers," Jerome continued.

Marty was usually good at reading people. Jerome DID seem like a candy freak, but he didn't seem like a thief. Marty decided to ask Mr. Dupont about his food critic job. Maybe Mr. Dupont needed to sample more candy than Mr. Hammond was willing to give.

The food critic talked into his tape recorder while he

interviewed Mr. Hammond. He asked how long he'd been in business (eleven years) and what his favorite candies were (mint wafers). When Mr. Dupont said the photographer should've been there by now, Mr. Hammond started to panic (again).

"The only jawbreakers she'll be able to take pictures of are empty display cases," Mr. Hammond whispered to Marty. "Why did I have to get robbed TODAY?"

Mr. Dupont told Mr. Hammond that the photographer knew what she was doing. "She's very creative," he said. "She'll have lots of ideas on how to photograph your spicy jawbreakers. The last piece we did together, she had the whole town involved."

Mrs. Bowman reappeared wearing a pair of wax candy lips. She took them out of her mouth and told Mr. Dupont he had to try her salted caramels too.

"You need to question her," Mr. Hammond whispered to Marty.

But Marty didn't have to question Mrs. Bowman because he'd just about solved the case.

AHA!

Marty headed outside with Mr. Hammond right behind him.

"You can't give up!" Mr. Hammond said. "You're the only detective I know."

But Marty wasn't giving up. He was finding the missing candy.

Marty hurried to the commotion at the fire station.

He gestured toward the firefighters in full uniform. They were holding a giant hose pretending to put out a fire— in a pyramid of candy jars filled with jawbreakers.

"No cause for concern—your candy's returned!" said Marty.

A woman with dark hair put down her camera and shook Mr. Hammond's hand. "I'm Lisa from the newspaper. Soon everyone in town will know about your fiery jawbreakers."

Mr. Hammond looked at the firefighters, the truck, and all the jars of candy.

These photos would bring in lots of business.

Lisa smiled when she saw Mr. Dupont.

I got here early and thought I'd set up. The firefighters helped me carry all the candy to the fire station.

Mr. Hammond apologized for not being there when Lisa arrived. He turned to Marty and asked him how he knew the photographer was involved.

"When I heard she was inventive, I became attentive." Marty knew fire trucks and sirens equaled something **HOT**.

Mr. Dupont took one of the jawbreakers. "Let's see if these things are as hot as everyone says."

Marty, Mr. Hammond, Lisa, and the firefighters watched as Mr. Dupont sucked on the jawbreaker. After a few moments, the critic's eyes began to water. Then his forehead started to sweat. Marty even thought he saw steam coming out of Mr. Dupont's ears.

Lisa grabbed the hose from the firefighter and aimed it at her friend. Marty didn't need his detective skills to see that Felix wasn't too happy getting soaked.

"You're still going to give me a good review, aren't you?" Mr. Hammond asked.

Mr. Dupont told Mr. Hammond these were the best spicy jawbreakers he'd ever had.

Lisa thanked the firefighters for their time and started to pack up the candy to take back to the store. She handed several jars to Jerome who had come to help.

Marty blocked Jerome's path.

I'm worried, Jerome. Are you taking those home?

Jerome told Marty not to worry, that he was definitely taking the candy back to Mr. Hammond's store.

"But I figure since I'm helping out,
I should at least get *one* jawbreaker
as a tip."

Marty thought that was a good idea
and popped one into his mouth too.

HOT! HOT!

HOT!

A JOB WELL DONE

Mr. Hammond fussed over the canisters of candy, making sure all were filled to the brim. When Mrs. Bowman came over from the comic book store, Mr. Hammond didn't throw her out. Instead he showed her the photos of the firefighters he'd taken with his phone.

Marty wondered if Mr. Hammond and Mrs. Bowman might end up being friends. He took the thank-you bag of

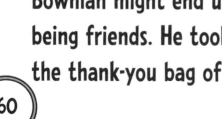

goodies from Mr. Hammond and headed home.

But before he did, he crossed the street and climbed up his favorite tree one more time.

There was only one thing better than sitting in a tree and that was sitting in a tree with a giant bag of candy.

3

THE CASE OF THE STOLEN POODLE

THE CRIME

When Marty got home, his sister, Katie, was doing her homework. The kitchen table was filled with piles of pennies, nickels, and dimes.

Katie counted out pennies as she worked. "Three plus seven equals ten," she said.

Marty swiped one of the pennies. "No disrespect, but your answer's incorrect."

Katie threw herself over the rest of the coins.

Stop messing around with my equation! I have a **test** tomorrow.

Marty was heading upstairs to play
video games when their neighbor Jackie
burst into the kitchen.

Darlene is **missing!** You have to help me find her!

Darlene was Jackie's poodle. Jackie
loved dressing up Darlene in sweaters and
bows and tiny shoes that Marty thought

were silly. He
wondered if
Darlene ran
away because
she didn't want

to be Jackie's canine doll anymore.

"Don't break a sweat—I'll find your
pet," Marty said.

"Oh, thank you, thank you!" Jackie did
a hula dance around the kitchen table
that made Marty want to hide inside the
cupboard.

But when you're a poet detective, you
don't say no to a new case.

SEARCHING FOR CLUES

Marty and his sister followed Jackie to her house. "There's a *Bobby the Bloodhound* marathon that Darlene and I were going to watch today. But our

television isn't working—I was trying to figure out how to tell Darlene."

Marty was having second thoughts about helping Jackie. But Jackie had lived in their neighborhood for years and was a good friend.

It was time to ask some tough questions.

"About Darlene—when was she last seen?"

Jackie told him she was getting ready to take Darlene for a walk when she realized her poodle had suddenly disappeared.

"What's that smell?" Katie asked.

Jackie led Marty and Katie into a kitchen full of goodies. Marty remembered that Jackie liked to cook and his mouth began to water when he saw the counter lined with tarts and quiches. (Here was another mystery—how could he possibly be hungry after eating so much candy that afternoon?)

Jackie took out plates for her friends. While the girls ate, Marty snooped around the house.

He found chew toys.

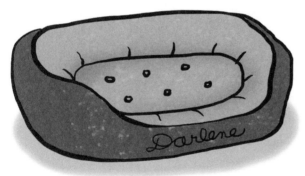

He found a dog bed.

He found dog food.

But no Darlene.

Marty spotted something sparkly. He reached underneath the shelf then held up his discovery for Jackie to see.

Put down your quiche—I found your dog's leash!

"That's because I hadn't slipped it on Darlene yet! Someone stole her, Marty!"

Marty was disappointed the leash wasn't a clue. He'd already solved two crimes today—would he be able to solve a third?

" **D**o you know anyone mean who would hurt Darlene?" Marty asked.

"Tina who lives next door *hates* Darlene," Jackie said.

Every time we pass her house, she insults my dog.

"Remember when she said poodles were the ugliest dogs ever?" Katie added.

"We should make sure she isn't the kidnapper."

Marty didn't tell his sister that kidnapping a poodle was actually *dog*napping. (Katie was not a detective, after all.)

The three friends marched over to Tina's. She opened the front door just a crack. Marty could hear a silly TV song playing in the next room.

Jackie told Tina that Darlene was missing.

Tina looked nervous. "Even if I knew where your dog was, I wouldn't tell you."

Marty pointed to something placed neatly on Tina's front steps.

Jackie stared at the mangled chew toy. "Yup—that's definitely the work of Darlene."

"Get that off my front steps!" Tina shouted.

Marty looked around the yard. If Darlene was here, did she come on her own or did someone bring her? And what was that silly music playing from inside Tina's house?

Sean the mail carrier came up the walk and asked what was going on. Marty was the first to answer.

"I want my dog back!" Jackie cried.

"I want another tart!" Katie shouted.

I want you all to leave! I haven't seen your silly dog.

Tina slammed the door.

"Um . . . I'm going to get back to work," Sean said.

But Marty wasn't done spying. Sticking out of the mail carrier's bag were some dog biscuits. Had he been the one to lure Darlene away from home?

THE SEARCH CONTINUES

Hee hee—
I see you!

Marty knew mail carriers often carried dog treats in their bags. He knew biscuits were a good way to bribe pets to stop barking. But Marty wondered if something else was going on. He hid behind cars and trees as he followed Sean on his route.

He watched Sean deliver a stack of mail to the pet shop.

Marty snuck behind the gerbil cages where the clerk was watching a show on the large TV. "Check this out," the clerk said to Sean.

He pointed to a terrier in a nearby cage. The terrier started howling at the *Bobby the Bloodhound* commercial.

All the dogs love Bobby.

Marty watched Sean go through the magazine rack. After a few minutes, he picked out an armload of magazines and took them to the cash register.

Sean was surprised when he looked up and spotted Marty.

Hey, junior detective—are you following me?

JUNIOR detective? Marty thought. **How insulting!**

Marty asked the mail carrier why he was buying poodle magazines. "That's a lot to read about one breed," Marty said.

"Jackie isn't the only one who loves poodles," Sean said. "I think they're great too."

Marty looked around.

I don't want to make a scene, but did *you* take Darlene?

"I would never steal someone's pet!" Sean said. "As soon as you said Darlene was missing, I started looking for her on my route. I'm buying these magazines for my girlfriend—she has a poodle too."

It was time for Marty to head back to Jackie's to say he had no leads.

"You sure you don't want to stay for the *Bobby the Bloodhound* marathon? It's starting now." The clerk pointed to the screen. "All the strays in town will be lined up to watch it."

Marty listened to the theme song and realized where he'd heard it before. He hurried out of the shop to tell Jackie the good news about her dog.

AHA!

Jackie and Katie were tearing apart the garage looking for Darlene. Marty almost tripped over a giant pile of board games in the middle of the driveway.

We didn't find Darlene but we found lots of games we forgot about.

Jackie looked even more panicked. "Do you think Darlene ran away because she doesn't love me anymore?"

Marty motioned for Jackie and Katie to follow him next door. They stood on tiptoes and looked through the window where Tina was sitting on the couch— watching TV with Darlene.

Jackie burst into the house.

You DID take my poodle!

Darlene's tail wagged as soon as she saw Jackie.

Tina looked up sheepishly. "I think Darlene knew your TV was broken and she brought me the bone because she wanted to watch *Bobby the Bloodhound*."

"I'm a sleuth—you should've told me the truth." Marty explained that he recognized the *Bobby the Bloodhound* theme song from when they talked to Tina earlier.

Tina wrinkled her nose and turned to Jackie. "Every time I see you and Darlene together, I get jealous. I want a dog so much but my parents won't let me have one."

"If you'd just invited us to watch

Bobby the Bloodhound with you, we would've come," Jackie said.

"Really?" Tina motioned to the rest of the couch. "Then have a seat!"

Katie ran back to Jackie's house and returned with a plate of tarts and quiches for them to share. (Even Darlene got one.)

Marty couldn't resist spending time with his friends—especially after solving the case. But you didn't need to be a poet detective to see what was going on between Darlene and *Bobby the Bloodhound*.

"Please don't blush, but Darlene's got a crush."

For the rest of the show, Marty watched Darlene staring at *Bobby the Bloodhound*. Her tail never stopped wagging.

A JOB WELL DONE

Marty's mom was stirring a large pot of tomato sauce at the stove when he and Katie got home.

Get out the confetti—we're having spaghetti!

"With meatballs and garlic bread," his mom added.

As he and Katie set the table, their mom asked them how they were doing.

"Just another day, keeping crime at bay," Marty answered.

Marty ran through the day's events: helping Nurse Laughlin, then Mr. Hammond at the candy store, followed by finding Jackie's poodle.

Today was busy for **ANY** poet detective.

He hoped tomorrow would be half as much fun. He'd be prepared to solve more mysteries— especially after a **giant** plate of spaghetti.